Dinosaurs in Love

Stella Businge

Greatness University Publishers
www.greatnessuniversity.co.uk

ISBN: 978-1-913164-63-8
ISBN-13: 978-1-913164-63-8

ABOUT THE AUTHOR

Stella Businge is the Author of *Ella and the Pink Creature*. She likes writing, reading, drawing, and gymnastics. She has a vivid imagination that allows her to tell her stories with great excitement. This book has been illustrated by Jumar Kwezi.

Dinosaurs in Love

Dinosaurs in Love

There was once a little friendly dinosaur named Fezzy. She lived with her mother Elle who loved her so much and was always fond of her.

Fezzy was a curious and brave little dinosaur who loved adventure. She always started her day willing to explore new places and find out about new things.

Fezzy's curiosity often led her into unknown places. Her mum was always worried about her getting lost. Fezzy's mother always told her to be home once it was getting dark.

Fezzy began each day with the same routine. She would wake up as soon as the sun came up. She would eat and then say to her mother, "I am off to find somewhere new, with a lot to see and do".

Fezzy's mother would reply the same response every morning, "Fezzy be safe. I love you so much. Come back to me when the sun stoops low." Fezzy would hop away, always ensuring that she told her mother, "I'll be safe, I love you always.

Fezzy's adventures took her far and wide. She loved venturing down to the swamp areas of water that she did not drink from.

This water area is where she

discovered new creatures such as turtles, frogs, and fish.

Fezzy loved meeting new friends.

Fezzy saw new plants such as reeds and lily pads. This new water area was a quiet place that she loved very much.

Fezzy explored the open fields that were far away. This is where she would see the open sky that stretched as far as her eyes could see.

She would also meet new creatures when she visited these flat stretches of land.

Some of the new creatures she met were cattle, prairie dogs, ground hogs, lions, zebras, baboons, hippos, and butterflies.

Fezzy enjoyed these flat stretches of land so that she could see the blue sky stretch for miles and miles. When there were clouds, she would watch them push across the sky as the wind blew. Fezzy loved the strong wind in her soft fur She loved the outdoors.

Fezzy went out one morning without thinking about where she was going. When she went out, she saw many new things as she traveled through the edges of the new forest Like lakes, rivers.

Fezzy spotted new butterflies, new insects, and new creatures. Fezzy was so delighted. She hopped faster and faster until she saw the sun beginning to set.

Suddenly, Fezzy stopped. She looked around and didn't know where she was. She was lost! At this point, Fezzy remembered what her mother always said to her, "If you get lost, do not move about, for I will come find you when the moon is out."

Fezzy did not listen to what her mum had told her. When she heard a voice calling, "Help! Help! Help me!", she ran into the nearby cave.

There, she saw a poor handsome blue dinosaur and he was shivering so much.

So, Fezzy took care of him. She also took some green big palm leaves and made a blanket for him. She asked him, "What is your name? Are you ok?" The blue dinosaur shouted," You need to go before the dangerous dragon comes. Thank you for your help." Fezzy said, No. I can't leave you". Fezzy insisted and pulled him out of the cave saying, "Tell me what is your name?" The blue dinosaur said, "My name is Ricky. I was hunting for food and the dragon came for me."

Just as they were reaching the entrance, the orange dragon came. They tried to run but the dragon caught them.

The dragon put Fezzy in a small cave.

The dragon was angry and said to them,

"Where do you think you are going?"

Fezzy said in a very courageous voice,

"We are going back to our homes. We

are not scared of you." The dragon got

so angry and his eyes turned red.

Smoke came out of his nose and the two small dinosaurs were so terrified. Fezzy fainted.

When Fezzy woke up, she looked around and she saw Ricky beside the edge of the cave.

Ricky said, "How are you my friend?"
Fezzy asked, "How did I get here?"
Ricky said, "I warned you about the
dangerous dragon." Then Fezzy asked,
"What is the name of this orange
dragon?" Ricky replied, "I don't know
his name".

Ricky asked, "what is your name by the way?" Oh, my name is Fezzy. What are we doing in this cave?"

Just when Fezzy had finished talking, the dragon came and laughed so loud. The dragon said, "You are my slaves". He opened the cage and said, "You are going out to get me food." Fezzy and Ricky went out of the cave.

The orange dragon was behind them while they were looking for food. It started to rain and they couldn't see the way.

The orange dragon started to find difficult to follow them and eventually got trapped in the tree.

So, Fezzy and Ricky stated running and found a boat.

At this point, Fezzy's mother found them. She got on the boat with them that took them to a faraway land.

The two friends got married on a beautiful sunny day and they lived happily ever after.

Dinosaurs in Love

Dinosaurs in Love Activities

Dinosaurs in Love

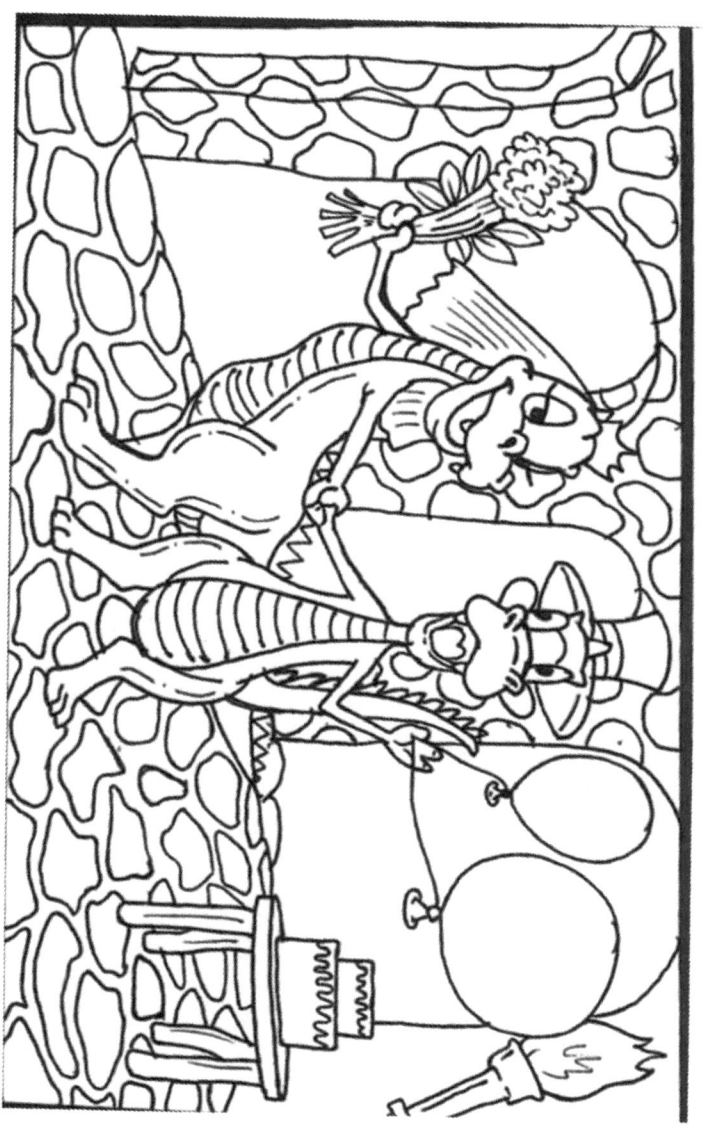

Dinosaurs in Love

Dinosaurs in Love

Dinosaurs in Love

Dinosaurs in Love

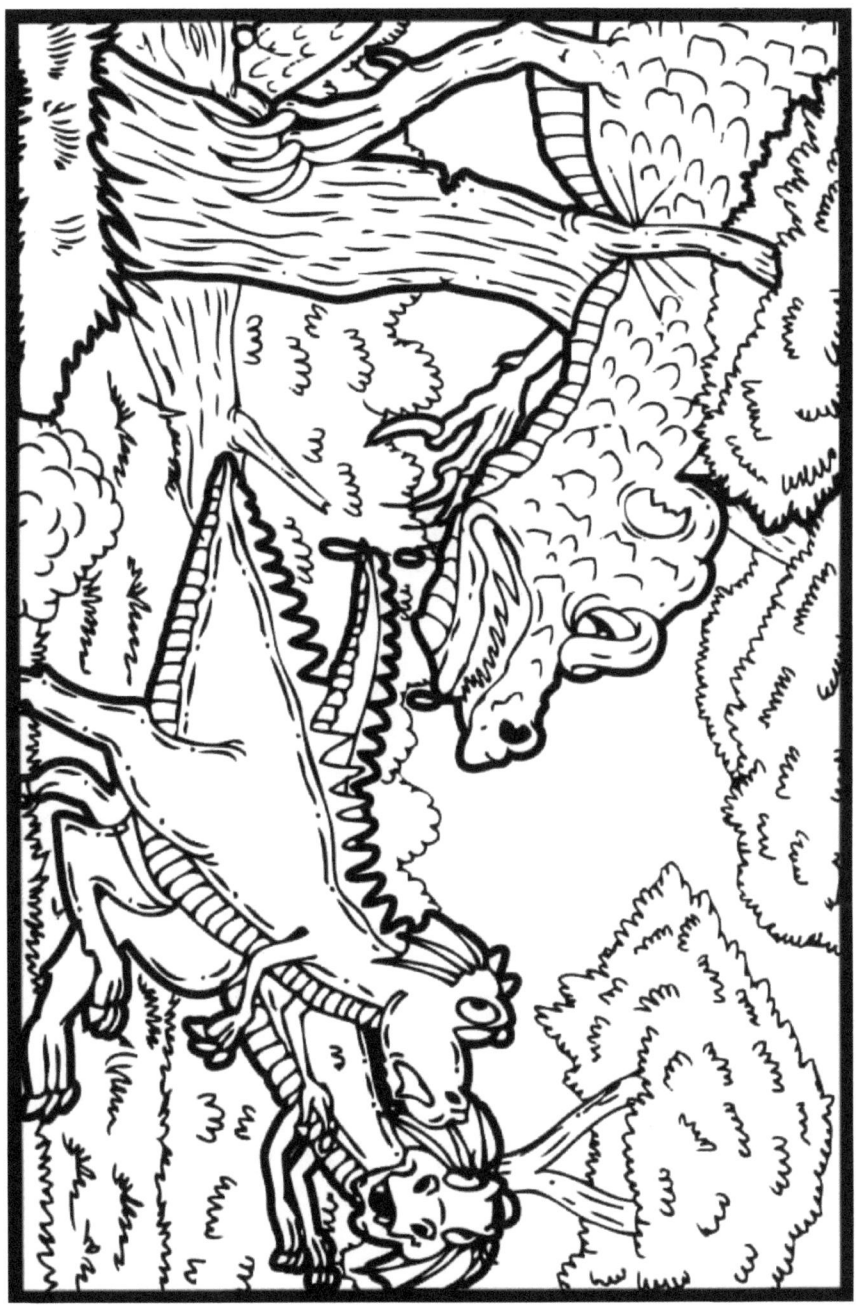

Dinosaurs in love

O	M	U	M	M	Y	E	L	B	L	O	W	H	U
G	S	E	H	S	S	E	E	O	S	S	L	U	U
O	I	V	E	O	O	S	T	A	C	T	G	N	M
W	A	A	S	R	M	M	R	T	R	U	N	T	G
A	A	C	T	A	E	S	E	K	R	A	S	I	N
D	L	R	G	N	W	A	E	S	W	A	A	N	I
I	O	H	B	G	H	F	I	F	G	I	I	G	R
N	V	M	O	E	E	E	Y	E	G	R	I	N	E
O	E	B	O	S	R	R	U	S	C	A	G	E	V
S	R	R	K	C	E	E	O	U	R	O	G	R	I
A	A	N	I	M	A	L	S	O	T	O	R	S	H
U	N	I	K	H	S	G	G	H	G	G	A	U	S
R	N	U	A	S	N	S	U	N	G	E	S	O	T
S	F	A	S	G	T	L	A	N	A	A	S	L	R

ORANGE
BOOK
MUMMY
CAVE
TREE
CAGE
HOUSE
HUNTING
RUN
SAFE
GRASS
LOVE
DINOSAURS
SHIVERING
SUN
ANIMALS
RAIN
SOMEWHERE
BOAT
LOW

word scramble

dinosaur in love

Look carefully at the jumbled words and try unscrambling as many words as you can.

Good luck!

oinasudr _____   baot _____   efzzy _____

ricyk _____   ifre _____   kinp _____

ulbe _____   oganer _____   eahnsomd _____

seavle _____   iarn _____   vace _____

mmu _____   lsot _____   obok _____

fienrds _____   banlols _____   yapph _____

nald _____   vole _____   waetr _____

teers _____   brsechna _____   grass _____

gace _____

Dinosaurs in Love

word scramble

dinosaur in love

Look carefully at the jumbled words and try unscrambling as many words as you can.

Good luck!

oinasudr **dinosaur**	baot **boat**	efzzy **fezzy**
ricyk **ricky**	ifre **fire**	kinp **pink**
ulbe **blue**	oganer **orange**	eahnsomd **handsome**
seavle **leaves**	iarn **rain**	vace **cave**
mmu **mum**	lsot **lost**	obok **book**
fienrds **freinds**	banlols **ballons**	yapph **happy**
nald **land**	vole **love**	waetr **water**
teers **trees**	brsechna **branches**	grass **grass**
gace **cage**		

GREATNESS UNIVERSITY PUBILISHERS

Greatness University Publishers is the natural choice for new authors, researchers, business people, religious leaders, celebrities, and diplomats.

Government departments, non-governmental organizations, churches, and royal families have also published their greatness with us.

Get in touch with us at greatnessuniversityuk@gmail.com and find out how to publish with us.

Dinosaurs in Love

www.ingramcontent.com/pod-product-compliance
Lightning Source LLC
Chambersburg PA
CBHW041031170626
46815CB00001B/44